T'

The Trouble With Phelim Fagan

by

John P. Warren

CONTENT WARNING!
This radio play contains themes of murder and
suicide as well as profanity. It is not suitable for
younger readers.

ISBN: 9798388630773

FX: denotes Sound Effects.

Set in rural Ireland in the present day.

SCENE 1

FX: A RADIO IS HEARD BEING
TUNED ACROSS THE AM RADIO
BAND. THERE'S THE SOUND OF
CRACKLING AND HUM UNTIL
A STATION WITH   MUSIC
PLAYING IS FOUND.

FX: THE MUSIC FINISHES
FOLLOWED BY A RADIO JINGLE
STATING THE STATION IS
CALLED "EMERALD 1170 AM."

PHELIM:

(with a sense of awe and wonder)

This must be a new radio station
on medium wave and it plays music
-- music that I like! Just listen to
how that unique AM sound sounds
like on my little radio. The quality
of the sound is different. To me

it's so pure and archaic but modern day music being broadcasted on it makes the music sound as if I've been transported to a higher plane. The artists sound like they have been exorcised by this oldest form of radio. Something like a transcendence from a mundane, ordinary existence to something that purifies their being but ultimately as escape in some mixed up way of using science and sound. I wish I could be a singer/songwriter and have my songs modulated in this way and experience this, but no, I guess I am a writer, well, trying to be.

SCENE 2

PHELIM IS AGAIN LISTENING TO THE RADIO STATION CALLED "EMERALD 1170."

PHELIM:

(distressed)

Will you just keep playing the music! Six months later and they're still playing the same old crap and talking nonsense right through the entire show.

<u>FX: THE MUSIC PLAYING ON
THIS STATION BEGINS TO
SOUND DISTORTED NOT BY
TECHNICAL REASONS BUT
BY HIS PSYCHOLOGICAL
CONDITION.</u>

PHELIM:

(annoyed, more distressed)

Not again!

<u>FX: HE CAN BE HEARD
GETTING UP FROM HIS CHAIR
AND SWITCHES OFF THE
RADIO ABRUPTLY. HE STARTS
MUMBLING TO HIMSELF.</u>

PHELIM:

I can't even listen to the fucking
radio anymore. I shouldn't have
thrown away my medication. Ah, I'm
heading into town.

<u>SCENE 3</u>

<u>FX: THE SOUND OF CARS
REVING CAN BE HEARD AND</u>

PHELIM'S FOOTSTEPS. HE IS
WALKING FAST.

A DOOR OPENS... IT SOUNDS
LIKE HE ENTERED A SHOP. THE
RADIO IS ON PLAYING MUSIC.

SHOPKEEPER:

How ya, Phelim? Long time no see.

PHELIM:

Could I get a box of cigarettes?

SHOPKEEPER:

Certainly, Phelim. Which ones do
you want?

PHELIM:

The cheapest.

FX: THE EMERALD 1170 AM
RADIO JINGLE PLAYS, AND, A
WOMAN'S VOICE SEEMINGLY
COMING FROM THE SPEAKER
OF THE RADIO CALLS OUT TO
HIM: "PHELIM!"

SHOPKEEPER:

Phelim, are you alright? You seem a little distant just now.

PHELIM:

It's that station.

SHOPKEEPER:

Emerald 1170? It's hard to believe that it's coming from a few miles away.

PHELIM:

What do you mean?

SHOPKEEPER:

I mean their transmitter is broadcasting from Morrison's Hill. Phelim, are you sure you're alright?

PHELIM:

I know where the damn station is broadcasting from!

(to himself)

Remember Phelim, that's where they

found him. Why is this happening?

SHOPKEEPER:

What's that, Phelim?

> FX: A CHORUS OF FEMALE
> VOICES CALLING OUT
> TO PHELIM BY HIS NAME
> FOLLOWED BY THEN A MORE
> MORBID SOUNDING MALE
> VOICE BEGINS TO SAY "PHELIM
> -- I KNOW WHAT YOU DID?"
> REPEATEDLY...

SHOPKEEPER :

Are you OK? Why are you blocking your ears like that?

> FX: PHELIM IS HEARD
> WALKING OUT AND THE SHOP
> DOOR CLOSES.

SHOPKEEPER:

(calling)

Phelim, you're cigarettes?

SCENE 4

FX: THE SOUND OF A RIVER
FLOWING AND BIRDS SINGING.

PHELIM:

(muttering to himself)

That radio station is haunting me. Siren female voices beckoning me to on the radio to enter the gates of hell. It must be sending out waves of evil energy, but how? Maybe it is being radiated from its transmitter site that's on cursed land or something.

(experiencing a realisation)

I shouldn't be so superstitious or am I delusional like that quack Mulhern calls it? But that has to be it! It's their transmitter! I know I'm right! That's the instrument which is blasting out those waves of evil from the source; the cursed ground is on condemning me my soul, my mind and body in this life and probably the next. OK, I've got to plan this out carefully. I've got to get to that transmitter before it gets me and before it takes my soul completely. You're a genius Phelim Fagan!

SCENE 5

FX: A CAR DOOR OPENING.

PHELIM:

Can I get a taxi?

TAXI DRIVER:

Certainly. Where to?

PHELIM:

The Emerald 1170 transmitter site on Morrison's Hill.

TAXI DRIVER:

That will be at least twenty euros each way.

PHELIM:

Here you go.

TAXI DRIVER:

Good man.

FX: PHELIM CLOSES THE CAR DOOR AND THE TAXI CAB

<u>ENGINE STARTS UP.</u>

<u>SCENE 6</u>

<u>FX: AS PHELIM IS EN ROUTE TO THE TRANSMITTER SITE. THE TAXI DRIVER IS HUMMING TO THE MUSIC ON THE RADIO.</u>

PHELIM:

What station is that you've on?

TAXI DRIVER:

It's the one that you going to see.

PHELIM :

Could you turn it off, please?

TAXI DRIVER:

Why?

PHELIM :

Ah... it reminds me of work that's all.

TAXI DRIVER:

Normally I don't allow nobody to tell

me what to do in my car, but they say the customer is always right.

THE TAXI DRIVER SWITCHES OFF THE RADIO.

PHELIM:

Thank you.

SCENE 7

FX: THE TAXI PULLS UP AND THE CAR DOOR CAN BE HEARD OPENING.

PHELIM:

Thank you. Come back for me in an hour.

FX: THE TAXI IS HEARD DRIVING OFF

PHELIM:

(to himself)

Here it goes.

FX: PHELIM'S FOOTSTEPS.

PHELIM:

> So that's the transmitter. Oh, I nearly forgot.
>
>> FX: HE IS HEARD RUSTLING THROUGH HIS BACK AND TURNS ON A POCKET RADIO.
>>
>> HE CAN BE HEARD TUNING THE RADIO SET UNTIL MUSIC IS PLAYING.

PHELIM:

> That's the station. Well, not for much longer.
>
>> FX: HE IS HEARD GOING THROUGH HIS BAG AGAIN AND A HEDGE CLIPPERS IS HEARD OPENING OUT LIKE IF WAS READY TO CUT SOMETHING..

PHELIM:

> (becoming distressed)
>
> Don't look back over there! That's where it happened. Poor Cyril.

(pauses for a moment)

Now where can I do the most damage, I wonder. Good job. I am wearing gloves. This cable here should be the power cable to the mast... here it goes.

ENGINEER:

What are you doing? Stop that right now! Tommy, call the Guards!

PHELIM:

(yelling over)

You don't understand! Your station has me damned!

ENGINEER:

You lunatic! What do you think you're doing?

PHELIM:

(angrily)

Don't call me a lunatic. I hate that word! This is evil ground and you're all evil!

<u>TOMMY IS TALKING TO THE ENGINEER.</u>

ENGINEER:

Look, son. The Guards will get you the help you need. Please come away from the cable otherwise you will be electrocuted. Come on, that's it, son.

<u>SCENE 8</u>

<u>FX: THE SQUAD CAR SIRENS AND THE SOUND OF AN AMBULANCE</u>

PHELIM:

(to himself)

I've failed in my mission. I'm cursed for life. You've really gone and done it now, Phelim. They are bringing me on a one-way trip to Benedict's.

<u>SCENE 9</u>

<u>THE HOSPITAL DOORS OPEN AND PHELIM'S TROLLEY CAN BE HEARD BEING WHEELED IN</u>

PHELIM:

(yelling)

I am a tormented Angel! Emerald 1170 is broadcasting from hell!

DOCTOR ERICA:

I'm going to have to give you something to help you relax.

PHELIM:

Keep away from me with that syringe!

PHELIM CAN BE HEARD STRUGGLING TRYING TO AVOID THE INJECTION.

PHELIM:

No! No. No. I feel so tired.

DOCTOR ERICA:

He's out. That was a fast acting sedative I just administered to him.

SCENE 10

DOCTOR
ERICA:

Welcome. Erica, is it?

Yes, Doctor Erica Phillips. I was recently assigned here at St. Benedict's.

DOCTOR
MULHERN:

Please, Erica, take a seat. It says here in your CV that you graduated first in your class.

DOCTOR
ERICA:

Yes, Doctor Mulhern.

DOCTOR
MULHERN:

Impressive. I take it you're here to discuss the readmission of Phelim Fagan?

DOCTOR

ERICA:

Yes, Doctor Mulhern. He hasn't been readmitted for over two years.

DOCTOR
MULHERN:

Haven't *re-offended* as I like top put it. Two months before he was readmitted here, I saw him as an outpatient. I prescribed him antipsychotics that he discontinued himself a few weeks ago and we're now in this situation. I want you to find out all you can from him. Get him to open up. He's twenty-four years old and resides a few miles from town. And is unemployed. I recently diagnosed him with the psychiatric condition of being schizo-affective and that has not changed as he underwent assessment this morning.

DOCTOR
ERICA:

He is suffering from paranoid delusions and auditory hallucinations; believing dark forces were calling out to him over the radio. One specifically directed at the station called Emerald 1170. When I asked Phelim about the evening he was admitted by the police, he became very upset.

DOCTOR
MULHERN:

(somewhat angrily)

May I remind you of your training, Erica? Do not get attached to this patient. Keep yourself distant.

DOCTOR
ERICA:

(taken aback)

You misunderstand me, Doctor Mulhern. I was simply empathizing with him.

DOCTOR
MULHERN:

Empathy leads to sympathy. Either way, you can't afford to show weakness to him otherwise he may just take advantage. I know him for a long time. He was an out-patient for years. Just don't let him get inside your head.

(pauses for a moment)

Look, I'm not without a heart. I just don't want to see any of my patients giving any of the staff the run around.

DOCTOR
ERICA:

I understand. That night, he was admitted. He was very agitated and delusional. Something about being a 'tormented angel.'

FX: DOCTOR MULHERN CAN BE HEARD TURNING PAGES OF HIS PATIENT'S FILE.

DOCTOR
MULHERN:

He yelled that his soul was being interfered by Emerald's radio transmitter. He was babbling this incoherently. We had to sedate him.

DOCTOR

ERICA:

He is resting now and becoming more lucid.

DOCTOR
MULHERN:

Good. Talk to him. Find out what's troubling him. Get him to open up. I want to know why he was possibly attempting to cause damage to that transmitter house outside his village. I have to admit that over the years I've come across some of the most outlandish of delusions but this certainly takes the biscuit. Speaking of which. Have your lunch, then I'll have him see you.

DOCTOR
ERICA:

Yes, Doctor Mulhern. Certainly.

DOCTOR
MULHERN:

Remember the advice I gave you?

FX: ERICA CAN BE HEARD
LEAVING DOCTOR MULHERN'S

OFFICE.

SCENE 11

DOCTOR
ERICA:

(joking)

Welcome, Phelim. Are you going to take notes on me?

PHELIM

(not amused)

What do you mean?

DOCTOR
ERICA:

I mean the pen and copy book that you have in your hands.

PHELIM

Oh, them -- I'm trying to write. But these damn tablets that ye have given me are suppressing my creative flow. It's like those little pieces of destruction create an extinguishing icy wave that envelops the fire in the parts of my mind that's creativity. My brain, because of your medication has left my mind like charcoal.

DOCTOR
ERICA:

Interesting. Phelim, this same medication will help you settle your thoughts. Your mind will become productive again. You're not the first patient I had who is also an aspiring writer and each of them has told me similar stories. All I'm saying is that writer's block is not as demystifying as it seems. Rest a while, slow down. It will come back.How long ago did you decide to take up creative writing or is it journalling you're doing?

PHELIM

(becoming agitated)

I really want to write everything before I forget it all!

DOCTOR
ERICA:

(soothingly)

What do you wish to write about, Phelim?

PHELIM:

I wish to write about my so-called pathetic life.

DOCTOR ERICA:

Where does your story begin?

PHELIM:

Like all stories, the beginning. I feel I have to tell my story because I look at the other people in my village and how life worked out for them and how it has been total bollocks for me. I think that gives me the unique position to tell this story, *my* story. My muse told me to say that.

DOCTOR ERICA:

Who is your muse?

PHELIM:

I see her in my visions. She is the inspiration that I desperately require.

DOCTOR
ERICA:

Your visions? Tell me more? Is that why you stopped your medication?

PHELIM:

I can't see her if I'm doped on that poison. They're blocking my creative side! When can I go home?

DOCTOR
ERICA:

You're very unwell, Phelim. And it's down to Doctor Mulhern. We can't force you to comply with resuming your medication, but it's a very good place to start.

PHELIM

I just told you why that I can't take them.

DOCTOR
ERICA:

We are aware of what you have said. You have a condition and as with most conditions like yours they are easily treated with suitable medication.

PHELIM:

(angrily)

I am not nuts! I write for god's sake!

DOCTOR
ERICA:

PHELIM:

Paranoia and Schizophrenia doesn't mean that, Phelim. Oh, it's that time.

Time for what?

DOCTOR
ERICA:

It's time for your afternoon tea session.

PHELIM:

Oh.

DOCTOR
ERICA:

I'll see you tomorrow.

FX: PHELIM CAN BE HEARD
GETTING UP AND OPENING
THE DOOR.

FX: HIS FOOTSTEPS CAN BE
HEARD AS HE PROCEEDS TO
THE CANTEEN.

SCENE 12

THE ACTION TAKES PLACE IN
THE COMMON AREA WHICH
IS ADJACENT TO THE NURSE'S
STATION, WHERE ERICA IS
PRESENT.

PHELIM ENTERS. ..

FX: RELAXATION MUSIC
PLAYING FROM A CD/RADIO
SET.

PHELIM:

(muttering to himself)

I hope they don't put on that station.

FX: PHELIM WALKING
PAST AN ELDERLY WOMAN
(MRS. MORIARTY) WHO IS
MUTTERING TO HERSELF.

MRS.
MORIARTY:

(to herself)

They'd have to leave a rubbish bin beside my bed right near my sore foot.

PHELIM:

Is that you, Mrs. Moriarty? How are you?

MRS.
MORIARTY:

(cranky)

Don't pass my sore foot!

FX: PHELIM FAILS TO HEAR MRS. MORIARTY'S REQUEST AND THE BIN CAN BE HEARD CHIMING AS PHELIM ACCIDENTALLY WALKS BESIDE IT AND HITS IT OFF MRS. MORIARTY'S FOOT.

MRS. MORIARTY:

Ah, my sore foot! What did you do that for?

PHELIM:

I'm sorry you cranky old witch!

FX: SHE CAN BE HEARD PICKING UP SOMETHING....

PHELIM:

Put that walking stick back down!

FX: THE SOUND OF PHELIM BEING STRUCK DOWN THE HEAD BY MRS. MORIARTY'S WALKING STICK.

PHELIM:

Ah, my head! You stupid bitch!

NURSE:

What's going on here? I'm alerting Doctor Mulhern.

DEREK:

Phelim, change that annoying music.

PHELIM:

I will not! And fuck off Derek!

DEREK:

Put it on to the radio. There's good music on Emerald 1170.

PHELIM:

Do not put that fucking station on. Their transmitter is only ten miles away! It will interfere with my soul!

DEREK:

What are you on about you dumb bastard, Fagan!

<u>FX: PHELIM CAN BE HEARD
ATTACKING DEREK.</u>

DOCTOR
MULHERN:

What's going on here? Nurse, sedate
Phelim Fagan and have him put in a
locked up ward 'till he learns how to
compose himself.

DEREK:

(shouting over at Phelim)

That's what you get, Fagan, for
saying I drank washing up liquid the
other day!

PHELIM:

(yelling)

You little bollocks. Derek! I never said
that!

DOCTOR
MULHERN:

Take him away now! You're going to
learn not to upset your other fellow

patients, Phelim.

SCENE 13

FX: THE RADIO IS PLAYING
A CONTINUOUS RECORDING
STATING THAT THE EMERALD
1170 FREQUENCY IS
RELAUNCHING WITH THE
COMMENCEMENT OF A BRAND
NEW RADIO STATION CALLED
"TRANSDRAMA AM":

RADIO
ANNOUNCER:

"This is a test transmission for
Transdrama AM. Your brand new
radio station for radio drama and
everything literary. We would like
to hear from you! If you would like
to submit work to our station for
consideration and have it potentially
broadcasted on this station, then go
to our website: transdrama-am.ie.

PHELIM:

(in shock)

Well, there goes all my favorite
music.

FX: THE RADIO'S VOLUME IS
RAISED.

DEREK:

(yelling)

Will you put some music on, Fagan?
That crap is boring me!

PHELIM:

Shut up, Derek! I want to hear this.

FX: THE RECORDING
BROADCAST ON THE RADIO IS
PLAYING:

RADIO
ANNOUNCER:

"This is a test transmission for
Transdrama AM. Your brand new
radio station for radio drama and
everything literary. We would like
to hear from you! If you would like
to submit work to our station for
consideration and have it potentially
broadcasted on this station, then go
to our website: transdrama-am.ie.

SCENE 14

DOCTOR
ERICA:

Phelim, How are you today?

PHELIM:

I don't like being locked like that with those others.

FX: THE DOOR CAN BE HEARD OPENING.

PHELIM

Oh no. What does *he* want?

DOCTOR
ERICA:

Doctor Mulhern is just going to observe your behaviour. There's nothing to worry about. I'll begin with a few questions.

PHELIM

He's here to find excuses to keep

me in that ward, I bet. You said questions. Just what questions? It looks like that he's testing you too.

FX: THE SOUND OF DOCTOR MULHERN WRITING NOTES WITH A PEN.

PHELIM

What's he writing about me?

DOCTOR
MULHERN

Just making notes. Nothing that you need to worry about.

DOCTOR
ERICA

How do you feel about people? Do you hate people, Phelim?

PHELIM:

Do you think I am a misanthrope? And judging by the surprise in your eyes that I actually came up with that fancy word. You're forgetting that I am an aspiring writer, Doctor Erica. But I can safely answer "no" to your question. I don't really hate anyone. If anything, I hate myself because I have this awkward condition being paranoid, as you've put it. Do you know what it feels like when your own people exclude you and you can't figure of why? Even at an early age, I was treated differently from everybody else because of my condition. It gave me the impression that I was inferior. It hurts when you endeavour to be normal only to be constantly shunned and excluded. The experts tell us that 'school is a microcosm of society'. I agree, as it got little better as I grew up.

DOCTOR
ERICA:

Do you remember what you told me the other day?

PHELIM

Yes, Doctor Erica, I told you a few days ago that I am a tortured angel. You see that's why other people torment me because I am really such a kind soul.

DOCTOR
ERICA:

You believe you're an 'angel' because you're subjected to torment and ridicule from above, or even God?

PHELIM:

No, the other one, -- the evil one. Don't say his name!

DOCTOR
ERICA:

I won't. I promise.

PHELIM:

He hates people who are intrinsically good by nature like angels are, so he tempts all the not so good people to carry out his dirty work like picking on me. And that's why I had to render Emerald 1170's transmitter inactive. He was using the energy from it to amplify people's hatred of me.

DOCTOR
MULHERN:

Remember, Phelim, that you have just broken the law and you're facing charges.

PHELIM:

Why can't you see that's there's more to this that meets the eye? Doctor Erica, here understands why all of this crazy crap happened to me. Mulhern, everything is with you is black or white but she sees the visible grey in between.

DOCTOR
MULHERN:

(losing his temper)

Don't lecture me, Phelim! It *is* a black and white situation -- you are suffering from a serious delusion because you neglected to take your medication and you caused criminal damage to a radio transmitter. This is very serious and I've had enough of your nonsense! You can't tell us one thing and have your private little war with the rest of humanity on the other!

FX: PHELIM CAN BE HEARD
STANDING UP.

DOCTOR
MULHERN:

Sit back down, Phelim! I'm not finished!

PHELIM:

(sighing)

Well, I am finished. Well Mulhern, did Doctor Erica here pass her test?

DOCTOR
MULHERN

(heard whispering)

I think we should increase his medication.

PHELIM

I heard that. And I can tell you now that there's no way I'm taking anymore of that poison.

DOCTOR

MULHERN

> You will do as I say. Now go back to your ward or I'll send you to a more secure unit.

PHELIM

> What?

DOCTOR
ERICA

> Just go, Phelim.

PHELIM:

> (in a smart accent)

> I'm going now! I'm going now! And I'm going to write all about this! I intend to send it along the way to the attention of the editor of this new radio station that's coming on air soon.

DOCTOR
MULHERN:

> Off with you.

PHELIM:

Just what kind of doctor are you?

DOCTOR
MULHERN:

The type of doctor who doesn't like his time wasted.

PHELIM:

To hell with you, Mulhern!

FX: PHELIM CAN BE HEARD MOVING TOWARDS MULHERN AND PUNCHING HIM IN THE FACE.

DOCTOR
MULHERN:

How dare you hit me? I'll see that they never let you home again!

DOCTOR
ERICA:

Oh, Phelim. Why did you do that?

FX: PHELIM CAN BEING RESTRAINED BY NURSES.

SCENE 15

FX: FOOTSTEPS CAN BE HEARD
AND A DOOR OPENS...

DOCTOR
ERICA:

Nurse, has he settled down?

NURSE:

Yes. Since the last two weeks, the meds that Doctor Mulhern prescribed him have helped with his delusions. He's no longer aggressive.

DOCTOR
ERICA:

Thanks. I've been off for the last two weeks. I'll have a chat with him now.

PHELIM:

Doctor Erica, it's you. I thought you were just a figment of my imagination.

DOCTOR
ERICA:

I'm just as real as you.

PHELIM:

I suppose Mulhern has thrown away the key and I'll never see the light of day ever again? But I've a play to write.

DOCTOR
ERICA:

(frustrated)

Phelim, do you really believe that any radio station will even look at anything you write especially considering your history?

PHELIM:

They have to. It's the only way that I can be exorcised.

DOCTOR
ERICA:

What?

PHELIM:

You heard me.

DOCTOR
ERICA:

I'll speak to Doctor Mulhern. You just focus on getting better.

PHELIM:

I will write and submit my work to them!

DOCTOR
ERICA:

That has to be a joke. You nearly damaged beyond repair the transmitter of a radio station and hit your consultant psychiatrist. All over what? I'll tell you why: because a few weeks before you were admitted here, you discarded your medication. As a result, you did those crazy things.

PHELIM:

You can't take this away from me! Or else there's only one thing I can do then.

DOCTOR
ERICA:

What's that?

PHELIM:

I end it all. There won't be anymore trouble from me then.

DOCTOR
ERICA:

Stop feeling sorry for yourself, Phelim. I know you enough that this's just one more of your ways of demanding attention.

PHELIM:

You think I'm lying?

DOCTOR
ERICA:

You will undergo a risk assessment, and then I'll determine whether you're being truthful.

PHELIM:

Well, I don't care about some stupid risk assessment. All I feel is nothing. I can't think and I can't feel thanks to those pills. Why do you think I destroyed them in the first place? Now I feel my mind shutting down as every second pass.

DOCTOR
ERICA:

What do you mean?

PHELIM:

I mean I can't think of anything else. I have one singular goal.

DOCTOR
ERICA:

I think I know what you mean. I can imagine what you're going through as I've heard it from other patients, but there's light at the end of the tunnel. If your meds are the issue, then we can look at suitable alternatives and we will keep you under observation.

PHELIM:

It's like a dark, cold tunnel where the light is dimming at every passing hour and now it is fully diminished altogether. What's the point?

DOCTOR
ERICA:

I get you well again so you can play your part in society when you're discharged..

PHELIM:

"Society," now that's something that I've never played a part in. It's like I am a dark moon spinning in a broken orbit of the society of planet Earth. How could I? I never had a job because no one will hire me. People see this schizo-affective condition in me and because I'm so self-conscious of my condition, they can see this vulnerability shining out through me and that repels them and gives them all the more reason to avoid me and treat me different. When my parents died, I was left all alone. I have no siblings. No wonder I blamed a radio station. I now know that what I did was preposterous, and I know I have to pay for it. Because of all those bad things I've done recently, well, let's just say it doesn't inspire me to continue on, especially if I can't redeem myself.

DOCTOR
ERICA:

And if you let me help you, Phelim? Will you at least try?

PHELIM:

I suppose I should think of any redemption as atonement. I'll try.

DOCTOR
ERICA:

That's what I want to hear.

PHELIM:

What about Mulhern? I assaulted him after all?

DOCTOR
ERICA:

I'll speak to him.

SCENE 16

DOCTOR
MULHERN:

(angrily, surprised)

What? You expect me to do nothing?

DOCTOR
ERICA:

Phelim is isolated and is suffering from alienation and isolation, and as a result he is suicidal. He is trying to swim in a turbulent ocean of agonizing distress. He can just about keep his head above the water. Those types of strong negative emotions are impacting him profoundly and make him amplify his delusions and paranoia such as believing himself to be imminently being possessed. He is extremely remorseful and I see this as an opportunity to be seized by him. I strongly believe he is on a path to change.

DOCTOR
MULHERN:

You're not forgetting, Doctor Erica, that he tried to shut down a radio station and not to mention my sore jaw.

DOCTOR
ERICA:

Please do this, Doctor Mulhern.

DOCTOR
MULHERN:

(pauses for a few moments)

This all goes against my better judgment, and I don't believe that this new way of thinking of yours is going to be effective for him or any other patient in Benedict's. But OK, we will try it your way for now. Don't forget that the radio station manager is calling. She wants to speak to Fagan when he's able to.

DOCTOR
ERICA:

Thanks, sir.

DOCTOR

MULHERN:

>Don't make me live to regret this.

SCENE 17

NURSE:

>Phelim, you have a visitor.

PHELIM:

>Who is it?

NURSE:

>It's your aunt.

PHELIM:

>Shauna?

SHAUNA:

>Phelim, can I see you?

PHELIM:

>Of course, Aunt Shauna.

SHAUNA:

>I'm so sorry that you ended up in

here like the way you did, but I suppose you sought help and you're getting it. I only wish my Cyril had somewhere like St. Benedict's to go to when he felt bad otherwise my son would be alive today.

PHELIM:

(distressed, in his own mind)

Stop! Will you stop! It wasn't my fault!

SHAUNA:

You seem somewhat distant. Are you alright, Phelim?

PHELIM:

(more distressed, in his own mind)

Shut up! It's not my fault!

SHAUNA:

I hope the food's nice here, Phelim. Are they feeding you well?

PHELIM:

(in his own mind)

Next, she'll say that she wishes Cyril got admitted here again.

SHAUNA:

If only we sent Cyril here!

PHELIM:

(aloud, yelling)

Shut up! I can't take this anymore!

SHAUNA:

What's wrong with you?

PHELIM:

Get her out of my sight now!

SHAUNA:

I won't stay where I'm not wanted.

NURSE:

Mrs. Fagan, it might be better if Phelim had time to himself.

SHAUNA:

I understand.

PHELIM:

Just get out! It wasn't my fault!

FX: FOOTSTEPS ALONG THE
CORRIDOR

DOCTOR
ERICA:

(concerned)

What's going on here? Why's he
upset?

NURSE:

His aunt stopped by. He was fine
before she came.

DOCTOR
ERICA:

Could you excuse us, Nurse?

PHELIM:

(in tears)

I don't want to talk about it, Doctor Erica. Just leave me alone.

DOCTOR
ERICA:

That's fine. I won't make you speak to me about anything that makes you feel uncomfortable.

PHELIM:

I should've helped him...

DOCTOR
ERICA:

Helped who?

PHELIM:

My cousin, Cyril.

DOCTOR
ERICA:

What happened to Cyril?

PHELIM:

It was a long time ago.

DOCTOR
ERICA:

Tell me anyway, please, Phelim.

PHELIM:

When Cyril and I were in secondary school, the other lads played a dirty trick on him. They set him up. He was always different, softer, gentle. He was autistic. One lunchtime the lads made out the teacher had called the men in the white coats to bring him off to the asylum. Cyril always feared that he would be locked up for life because our uncle spent all his life here in Benedict's and died here. That was the one thing he feared, so one day he took control of his own life.

DOCTOR
ERICA:

What do you mean?

PHELIM:

He did himself in on Morrison's Hill.

DOCTOR
ERICA:

That's awful, but it's not your fault, Phelim.

PHELIM:

Oh, yes, it is *my* fault. I was not there for Cyril in his hour of need. I actually felt like he deserved the slagging just because of the way he was. He let me down, and I was ashamed to be related to him as he embarrassed me.

DOCTOR
ERICA:

In what way would Cyril embarrass you, Phelim?

PHELIM:

He would talk about childish things and show me up in front of my friends and girls. I feel like such a bad person. You know, when you think about it all, I deserve all this. It's my karma.

DOCTOR
ERICA:

It still doesn't make it your fault. You can't help the way you think. Did you tell Cyril about the way you felt about him being autistic?

PHELIM:

No, never. It was all deep down in the dark recesses of my mind. I was never against Cyril, really. I left him out and cut him out of my mind.

DOCTOR
ERICA:

Then he will never know.

PHELIM:

No, I suppose not.

DOCTOR
ERICA:

(realisation)

That's been the trouble all along, hasn't it?

PHELIM:

What do you mean?

DOCTOR
ERICA:

I mean, your cousin Cyril dying by suicide on Morrison's Hill and the subsequent delusion you experience regarding that place. Cyril wasn't the only issue that you 'cut out' of your mind, was it?

DOCTOR
ERICA:

Think about it. You also blocked off the bad memories of the time in and leading up to his death and then especially the place called Morrison's Hill.

PHELIM:

Morrison's Hill?

DOCTOR
ERICA:

Yes. Morrison's Hill represented to

you a place of such untold suffering to you and Cyril that you found fault in the transmitter located there.

PHELIM:

(surprised)

What has this got to do with me trying to damage Emerald 1170's transmitter?

DOCTOR ERICA:

It's not uncommon for people who have undergone deep traumatic events to suppress memories of this trauma in the way you have done, Phelim. This kind of memory suppression can cause mental breakdown like you've experienced. Plus, blocking off strong emotions related to all of this can cause enormous stress on your mind.

PHELIM:

I'm tormented, but no angel.

DOCTOR ERICA:

You must learn to forgive yourself, Phelim.

PHELIM:

Yes, and others too.

DOCTOR
ERICA:

I came here today because Doctor Mulhern is thinking of discharging you on probation. You have demonstrated good behaviour over the last few days and we would want to see how you would get on back out living in the general community. You will have to agree to visitations from your key worker and agree to attend out patients once a week. What do you think, Phelim?

PHELIM:

Okay, I agree. I need to get back home and begin writing my story. Thanks, Doctor Erica! But, I thought my outburst with my aunt would hinder my release?

DOCTOR

ERICA:

That was an healthy expression of strong built up emotions. It's tea time out in the canteen. Have a cup.

PHELIM:

OK.

SCENE 18

FX: A TAXI'S DOOR CAN BE HEARD CLOSING.

NURSE:

Goodbye, Phelim.

PHELIM:

(under his breath)

And goodbye to you all too. Hope to never see any of you ever again.

SCENE 19

FX: THERE ARE BIRDS SINGING AND FOOTSTEPS CAN BE HEARD FOLLOWED BY SOMEONE INSERTING A KEY

AND UNLOCKING A DOOR.

PHELIM:

(to himself)

Ah, home sweet home.

HE SWITCHES ON THE
RADIO AND BEGINS TO
LISTEN TO THE SAME TEST
TRANSMISSION FOR THE
TRANSDRAMA RADIO
STATION.

PHELIM:

Now, all I have to do is write and there has to be a way that I can submit my story to this new radio station.

(becoming regretful)

Why did I do what I did to that transmitter? I have ruined it all on myself. All because of what they did to poor Cyril. They, it seems, have taken my future away from me too. I can never do this now. Oh, why did I become obsessed with stupid AM radio. What was I thinking? I need a drink.

SCENE 20

THE LOCAL PUB. PEOPLE CAN
BE HEARD LAUGHING AND
TALKING.

PHELIM WALKS IN.
EVERYTHING GOES SILENT
UNTIL DEREK CAN HEARD
BOASTING ABOUT SOMETHING
HE DID IN THE PAST TO HIS
FRIENDS.

PHELIM:

Derek? Did you get released too?

DEREK:

I sure did. It's good to be away from
those lunatics.

(gloating, to his friends)

You should've seen the look on that
retard's on face.

PHELIM:

The look on whose face?

DEREK:

Never mind, Fagan.

PHELIM:

Derek, are you speaking about my cousin, Cyril?

DEREK:

What about it, Fagan?

PHELIM:

Take it back!

DEREK:

I will not because I don't have to do anything you say.

PHELIM:

It was *you?* Wasn't it Derek?

DEREK:

I don't know what you're talking about.

PHELIM:

It was you who set up poor Cyril?

DEREK:

So, if I did. He got what he deserved because he was too slow to cop on.

PHELIM:

I'll kill you!

BARMAN:

Hold on right here the both of ye!

DEREK:

He said he was going to kill me. He threatened me!

PHELIM:

It was him! It was all his idea. He set up Cyril all those years ago.

DEREK:

So. God's on my side. Cyril Fagan was much too stupid like his cousin here. You both don't count.

PHELIM:

No, Derek. You're the one that has something missing up there.

SCENE 21

IT'S OUTSIDE, LATER ON THAT EVENING.

FX: PHELIM CHARGING TOWARDS DEREK...

DEREK:

What do you want, Phelim? You know, I really hate the sight of you.

PHELIM:

I know you hate me because I remind you of what you did to Cyril.

DEREK:

Yeah, both of you are annoying, bad little memories. More like I remind you of your failure to have helped him when you should've had.

PHELIM:

This is for Cyril!

FX: PHELIM'S HEARD STABBING
DEREK...

PHELIM:

(raging)

That's for my cousin!

SCENE 22

FX: THE HOSPITAL ALARM
GOES OFF...PHELIM IS BEING
READMITTED BY THE GUARDS.

DOCTOR
MULHERN:

Nurse, what happened?

NURSE:

Phelim Fagan stabbed Derek Miller in
town earlier this evening.

DOCTOR
MULHERN:

Is he alright?

NURSE:

An ambulance came to his aid.

DOCTOR
MULHERN:

Where's Fagan now?

NURSE:

In a secure unit.

DOCTOR
MULHERN:

I'll see that he never sees the off
outside day ever again!

SCENE 23

DOCTOR
MULHERN:

Now, Ms. Phillips, do you see what
your new age style of professional
thinking has achieved? They
couldn't save Derek Miller last night.
He passed away in the ambulance on
their way to A and E.

DOCTOR
ERICA:

I just don't know what to say... I genuinely believed that Phelim Fagan was on the road to a meaningful recovery so he could one day become a productive member of society.

DOCTOR
MULHERN:

That's just more of it. I expect a full report followed by your immediate resignation.

SCENE 24

FX: A DOOR CAN BE HEARD OPENING...

NURSE:

Doctor Erica, good morning. I hear you're off to pastures new?

DOCTOR
ERICA:

Yes. It's back to university for me.

NURSE:

I want to tell you I and the rest of the nursing staff will really miss you.

DOCTOR
ERICA:

Thanks. That's nice to hear. Is he in there?

NURSE:

Yes. The Guards just left ten minutes ago. St. Benedict's has made national headlines. All thanks to Mister Fagan here.

DOCTOR
ERICA:

Do you mind accompanying me?

NURSE:

I certainly wouldn't have you see him alone.

FX: FOOTSTEPS.... AS THEY
ENTER PHELIM'S ROOM.

DOCTOR
ERICA:

Phelim, I need to ask you one question?

PHELIM:

And I can guess what that all important question is.

DOCTOR
ERICA:

No doubt you can. Why?

PHELIM:

Why did I take Derek Miller's life from him?

DOCTOR
ERICA:

Yes, why Phelim? Why did you do that awful act?

PHELIM:

Because he ended Cyril's life and ruining mine. My own life ended a long time ago thanks to everything I did wrong throughout my life. It was all down to him. People throughout all my life put in a box just because of how they would perceive me and not only that they had the audacity to expect me to behave in that way they saw me. If I ever tried to do something different say improving myself -- they'd see it as me behaving strangely or out of character or in fact deviating from the way they thought how they knew me. Cyril had that trait in common with me and they did the same to him only he wasn't as strong as me. I was determined to show everyone that there's more to me than met the eye.

DOCTOR
ERICA:

Like becoming a writer?

PHELIM:

Yes. But I guess it's too late for all that now.

DOCTOR
ERICA:

Oh, Phelim. That doesn't give you the right to self-appoint yourself as judge, jury and executioner. Now

I really fear for you and the life you now have condemned yourself to. Goodbye Phelim. I hope you can make sense of it someday and find some kind of peace for yourself.

SCENE 25

IT'S NIGHTTIME...

FX: THE SOUND OF RAIN AND THUNDER AS THERE IS A WEATHER STORM OUTSIDE.

FX: THE SOUND OF SOMEONE RUNNING ALONG THE CORRIDOR...

NURSE:

(yelling)

Phelim! Get back here!

Where's has he gone?

SCENE 26

FX: THE SOUND OF PHELIM WALKING THROUGH FIELDS. CATTLE AND SHEEP ARE MOOING AND

BLEATING...WHILE THE STORM
CONTINUES.

PHELIM:

(distressed)

I know it's somewhere up here! Not far now.

FX: THUNDER...

PHELIM:

(relieved)

At last. Faithful Morrison's Hill. That's where poor Cyril did it. Well, I can tell him I vindicated him and me.

FX: THE SOUND OF PHELIM STRUGGLING AGAINST THE HAZARDOUS WEATHER AROUND HIM.

PHELIM:

Well, here it goes!

FX: THE SOUND OF PHELIM JUMPING AND LANDING HARSHLY ON STONY GROUND.

SCENE 27

FX: A DOOR OPENS...

NURSE:

Good luck, Doctor Erica and thanks for everything.

FX: THE SOUND OF SOMEONE WALKING URGENTLY ALONG THE CORRIDOR...

DOCTOR
MULHERN:

Doctor Erica, can I see you before you leave?

DOCTOR
ERICA:

Certainly, Doctor Mulhern.

FX: THEY ENTER ANOTHER ROOM. THE DOOR IS CLOSED SHUT.

DOCTOR
MULHERN:

Phelim Fagan died last night. It was by suicide.

DOCTOR
ERICA:

How?

DOCTOR
MULHERN:

He somehow escaped from here and make his way out to Morrison's Hill. He died in the same way as his cousin Cyril did.

DOCTOR
ERICA:

Poor Phelim. He was such a tortured soul. He grew up disadvantaged in so many ways. Not only had he a debilitating psychiatric condition that others saw he had and that just resulted in him being subjected to isolation and stigma and not to mention crippling self guilt.

DOCTOR
MULHERN:

I suppose he was blessed by a curse or two. If only I had prior knowledge of Derek Miller and that dreadful history between the two of them. At least I know he can't hurt anyone else now.

DOCTOR
ERICA:

No, he can't and nobody can hurt him either anymore.

THE END.

Printed in Great Britain
by Amazon

20522373R00048